Sweet Strawberries

STORY BY **PHYLLIS REYNOLDS NAYLOR**

PICTURES BY **ROSALIND CHARNEY KAYE**

ATHENEUM BOOKS FOR YOUNG READERS

Atheneum Books for Young Readers
An imprint of Simon & Schuster Children's Publishing Division
1230 Avenue of the Americas
New York, New York 10020

Book design by Angela Carlino
The text of this book is set in Berkeley Bold.
The illustrations are rendered in collage, oil and acrylic.

Printed in the United States of America

First Edition
10   9   8   7   6   5   4   3   2   1

Library of Congress Cataloging-in-Publication Data:
Naylor, Phyllis Reynolds.
Sweet strawberries / story by Phyllis Reynolds Naylor ; pictures by Rosalind Charney Kaye.—1st ed.
p.   cm.
Summary: A wife and her grumpy husband go to market.
ISBN 0-689-81338-4 (alk. paper)
[1. Strawberries—Fiction. 2. Markets—Fiction.] I. Kaye, Rosalind Charney, ill. II. Title.
PZ7.N24Sr   1999   [E]—dc21   97-48411

To Jennifer Altemus, with love
—P. R. N.

To Ken, with a thousand unspoken words of gratitude
—R. C. K.

A man was taking his fish to market, and his wife was
going along.

He wasn't the worst man in the world, but he wasn't the nicest, either. The woman had been his wife for a good long time, however, so she was used to his ways.

After he had helped her into the wagon, his wife said, "I do hope they have strawberries, plump and sweet. I haven't had strawberries for many a month."

"Complain, complain!" the man grumbled. "All you do is complain."

"It was only a thought," said his wife.

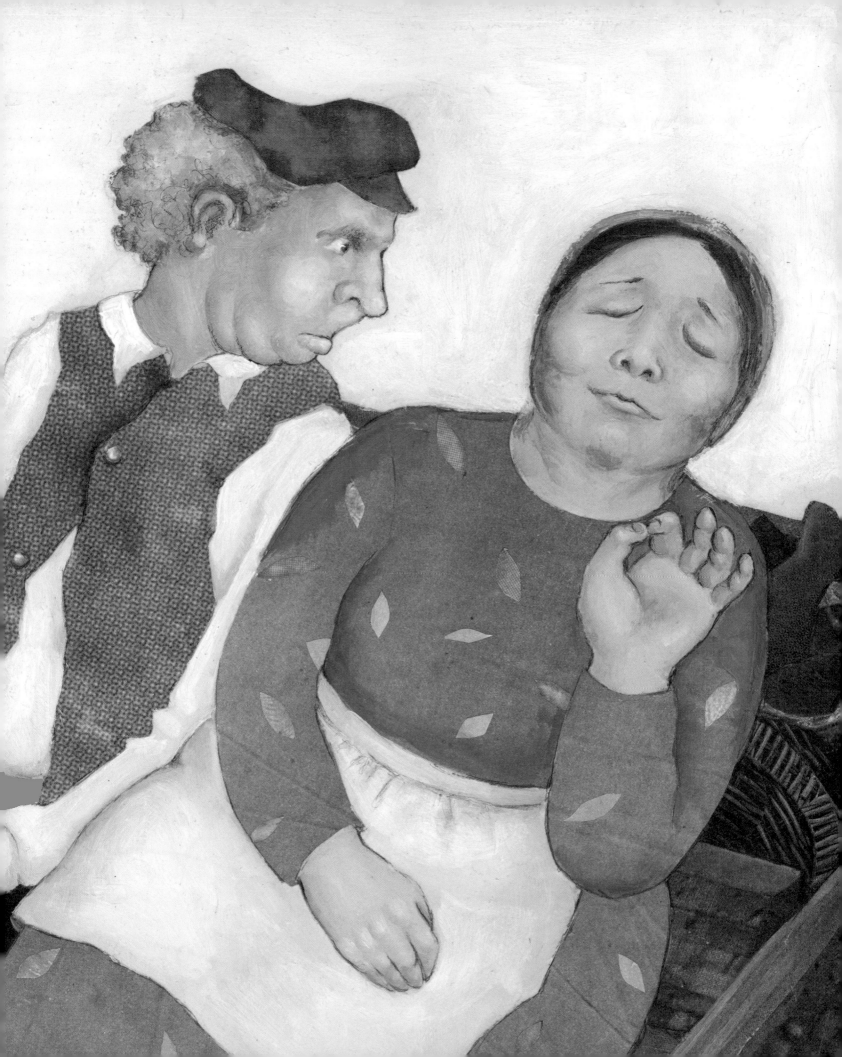

As they rounded the bend, a young lass herded her flock of geese across the road. The horse had to stop, and the man grew restless.

"Why didn't you wait till we had gone by?" he called gruffly.

"My dear," said his wife, "she is just a young girl."
"She is too impatient," said her husband. "Always in a hurry."

When they came to the village, the boy who tended the gate had fallen asleep.

The man did not want to get down out of the wagon, and shouted, "Here, boy! On your feet!"

"My dear," said his wife, "he is just a young lad."

"He is the laziest boy I ever saw," said her husband.

As the man turned his horse toward the shade of a tree, a farmer with five children pulled his wagon in first.

"You selfish oaf!" the man yelled at the driver. "Didn't you see I was going to put my own wagon there?"

"My dear," said his wife, "that farmer has a wagonload of children needing shade."

"That was my spot," said her husband. "I park there every market day."

The man traded his basket of fish for a bag of flour, but when he found that the sack wasn't full, he cried angrily, "You cheat me, Sir! Fill my bag to the top!"

"My dear," said his wife, "the merchant is old and his eyesight is poor. The sack is *almost* full."

"He is as stingy as they come," said her husband.

The man and his wife walked about the market, looking at round yellow apples and beans of the brightest green.
On a table just ahead were some strawberries, plump and red.

"Please, let us buy some," the wife begged. "I have never seen strawberries so big and ripe." Her mouth ached at the sight of them; she could almost taste their sweetness on her tongue.

But her husband shook his head. "They cost too much, far too much," he said.

At that, his wife cried out, "You are the most stingy, selfish, lazy, impatient, complaining man I have ever seen!"
And she climbed back into the wagon and refused to talk.

Now the man had been her husband a good long time, but he had never seen her like this. Surely all the unpleasant people they had met that day had simply upset her.

So on the way home, he whistled to the birds to cheer her: "Wheeta whee! Wheeta whee!"
His wife folded her arms and said nothing.

The man sang to his horse:
"Hey ho, hi ho,
Trot along the road, so."

His wife simply looked the other way.

So the man stood up in the wagon and did a little dance
as he drove: *Tappity tap! Clackity clack!*
But his wife said nothing at all, and didn't even smile.

Once they were home, however, they went about their work as usual, and life went on as before.

The next Saturday, when the man and his wife set out for market, the man hoped they would not meet any lasses in a hurry, any lazy lads, any selfish oafs or stingy tradesmen. He did not want his wife upset again.

When he saw the girl with the geese, he slowed his horse
and called out,
  "Fine day to you, Miss!"
The lass, very much surprised, smiled at him and said,
  "And to you, good Sir!"

When they came to the village and found the boy asleep
again, the man sang at the top of his lungs:
    "Hi dee dee ho!
    Hi dee dee hey!"

The boy awoke and, grinning, jumped up and opened the gate.

Once again the man discovered that someone had taken his favorite place beneath the tree, but he said, "Ah, well. One tree is as good as another, eh?" and parked his wagon somewhere else.

And this time, he traded his fish for the largest basket of
strawberries his wife had ever seen.

The two sat down on the grass to enjoy them then and there,
and people waved as they passed.

"Isn't it remarkable how everyone has changed so in only a week?" the man asked his wife in surprise.

And the woman, who had been his wife for a good long time, just smiled and said nothing. Her husband wasn't the nicest man in the world, she knew, but he wasn't the worst one either.